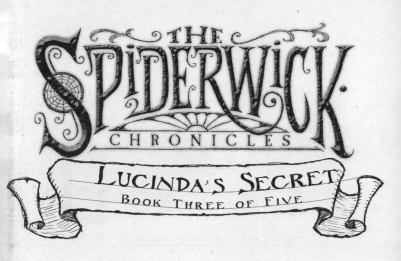

THE SPIDERWICK CHRONICLES

LUCINDA'S SECRET

BOOK THREE OF FIVE

Tony DiTerlizzi *and* Holly Black

Simon and Schuster

London New York Sydney Toronto New Delhi

SIMON & SCHUSTER

First published in Great Britain by Simon & Schuster UK Ltd, 2003
A CBS COMPANY

This edition published in 2018

Originally published in the USA in 2003 by Simon & Schuster Books
for Young Readers, an imprint of Simon & Schuster
Children's Division, New York.

Copyright © by Tony DiTerlizzi and Holly Black, 2003
Book design by Tony DiTerlizzi and Dan Potash.

1 3 5 7 9 10 8 6 4 2

Simon & Schuster UK Ltd
1st Floor, 222 Gray's Inn Road
London WC1X 8HB

A CIP catalogue record for this book is available
from the British Library

ISBN 978-1-4711-7496-4

Printed and bound by CPI Books (UK) Ltd, Croydon, CR0 4YY

For my grandmother, Melvina,
who said I should write a book just like this one
and to whom I replied that I never would
—H. B.

For Arthur Rackham,
may you continue to inspire others
as you have me
—T. D.

Table of Contents

List of Full-Page Illustrations

Dear Reader,

Over the years that Tony and I have been friends, we've shared the same childhood fascination with faeries. We did not realize the importance of that bond or how it might be tested.

One day Tony and I—along with several other authors—were doing a signing at a large bookstore. When the signing was over, we lingered, helping to stack books and chatting, until a clerk approached us. He said that there had been a letter left for us. When I inquired which one of us, we were surprised by his answer.

"Both of you," he said.

The letter was exactly as reproduced on the following page. Tony spent a long time just staring at the photocopy that came with it. Then, in a hushed voice, he wondered aloud about the remainder of the manuscript. We hurriedly wrote a note, tucked it back into the envelope, and asked the clerk to deliver it to the Grace children.

Not long after, a package arrived on my doorstep, bound in red ribbon. A few days after that, three children rang the bell and told me this story.

What has happened since is hard to describe. Tony and I have been plunged into a world we never quite believed in. We now see that faeries are far more than childhood stories. There is an invisible world around us and we hope that you, dear reader, will open your eyes to it.

HOLLY BLACK

Dear Mrs. Black and Mr. DiTerlizzi:

I know that a lot of people don't believe in faeries, but I do and I think that you do too. After I read your books, I told my brothers about you and we decided to write. We know about real faeries. In fact, we know a lot about them.

The page attached* to this one is a photocopy from an old book we found in our attic. It isn't a great copy because we had some trouble with the copier. The book tells people how to identify faeries and how to protect themselves. Can you please give this book to your publisher?

If you can, please put a letter in this envelope and give it back to the store. We will find a way to send the book. The normal mail is too dangerous.

We just want people to know about this. The stuff that has happened to us could happen to anyone.

Sincerely,

Mallory, Jared, and Simon Grace

*Not included.

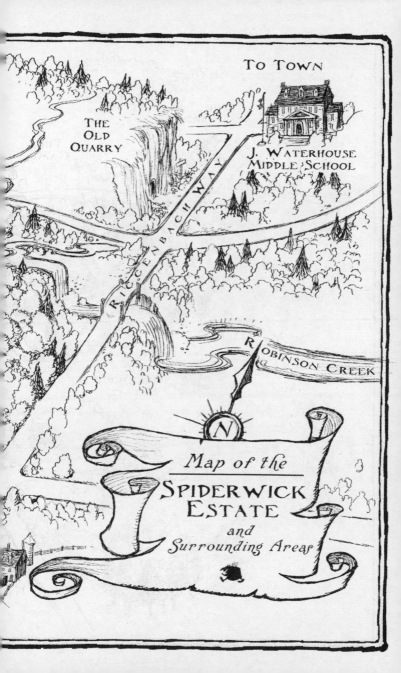

Turned it inside out.

Chapter One

IN WHICH Many Things Are Turned Inside Out

Jared Grace took out a red shirt, turned it inside out, and put it on backward. He tried to do the same with his jeans, but that was beyond him. *Arthur Spiderwick's Field Guide to the Fantastical World Around You* lay atop his pillow, open to a page on protective devices. Jared had consulted the book carefully, not sure any of it would help much.

Since the morning after the Grace kids had returned with the griffin, Thimbletack had been out to get Jared. Every so often he could hear the little brownie in the wall. At other times

Jared thought he saw him out of the corner of his eye. Mostly, though, Jared just wound up the victim of some new prank. So far his eyelashes had been cut, his shoes had been filled with mud, and something had urinated on his pillow. Mom blamed Simon's new kitten for the last, but Jared knew better.

Mallory was completely unsympathetic. "Now you know how it feels," she kept saying. Only Simon seemed at all concerned. And he practically had to be. If Jared hadn't forced Thimbletack to give up the seeing stone, Simon might have been roasted over a spit in a goblin camp.

Jared tied the laces of his muddy shoe over an inside-out sock. He wished that he could find a way to apologize to Thimbletack. He'd tried to give back the stone, but the brownie hadn't wanted it. The thing was, he knew that if everything were to happen all over again, he would do exactly what he had done. Just thinking about Simon being held by goblins—while Thimbletack stood around talking in riddles—made Jared angry enough to almost break his laces with the force of the knot.

"Jared," Mallory called from downstairs. "Jared, come here a minute."

He stood up, tucking the Guide under his arm, and took a step toward the stairs. He fell immediately, hitting his hand and knee against the hardwood floor. Somehow Jared's shoelaces had been tied together.

Downstairs Mallory was standing in the kitchen, holding a glass up to the window so that the water caught the sunlight and cast a rainbow

The water caught the sunlight.

on the wall. Simon sat next to her. Both of Jared's siblings seemed transfixed.

"What?" Jared said. He was feeling grumpy and his knee hurt. If all they wanted was to show him how pretty the stupid glass looked, he was going to break something.

"Take a sip," Mallory said, handing the glass to him.

Jared eyed it suspiciously. Did they spit in it? Why would Mallory want him to drink water?

"Go ahead, Jared," Simon said. "We already tried it."

The microwave beeped and Simon jumped up to remove a giant mound of chopped meat. The top part was a sickly gray, but the rest of it still looked frozen.

"What's that?" Jared asked, peering at the meat.

"For Byron," Simon said, dumping it into a

huge bowl and adding corn flakes. "He must be getting better. He's always hungry."

Jared grinned. Anyone else would be wary of a half-starved griffin recuperating in their carriage house. Not Simon.

"Go on," Mallory said. "Drink."

Jared took a sip of the water and choked. The liquid burned his mouth and he spat half of it onto the tile floor. The rest slid down his throat like fire.

"Are you crazy?" he yelled between bouts of coughing. "What was that?"

"Water from the tap," Mallory said. "It all tastes that way."

"Then why did you make me *drink* it?" Jared demanded.

Mallory crossed her arms. "Why do you think all this stuff is happening?"

"What do you mean?" Jared asked.

"I mean that weird things started happening when we found that book, and they're not going to stop until we get rid of it."

"Weird stuff was happening before we found it!" Jared objected.

"It doesn't matter," Mallory said. "Those goblins wanted the Guide. I think we should

give it to them."

The room was silent for a few seconds. Finally Jared managed a hushed, "What?"

"We should get rid of that stupid book," Mallory repeated, "before someone gets hurt — or worse."

"We don't even know what's wrong with the water." Jared glared at the sink, anger coiling in his gut.

"Who cares?" Mallory said. "Remember what Thimbletack told us? Arthur's field guide is too dangerous!"

Jared didn't want to think about Thimbletack. "We need the Guide," he said. "We wouldn't have even known there was a brownie in the house without it. We wouldn't have known about the troll or the goblins or anything."

"And they wouldn't know about us," Mallory said.

"It's mine," Jared said.

"Stop being so selfish!" Mallory shouted.

Jared clenched his teeth. How dare she call him selfish? She was just too chicken to keep it. "I decide what happens to it, and that's final!"

"I'll show you *final.*" Mallory took a step toward him. "If it wasn't for me, you'd be dead!"

"So?" Jared said. "If it wasn't for me, *you'd* be dead right back!"

Mallory took a deep breath. Jared could almost imagine steam coming out of her nose. "Exactly. We could all be dead because of that book."

The three of them looked down at "that book" dangling from Jared's left hand. He turned to Simon, furious. "I suppose you agree with her."

Simon shrugged uncomfortably. "The Guide did help us figure out about Thimbletack and

9

"We need the Guide."

about the stone that lets you see into Faerie."

Jared smiled in triumph.

"But," Simon went on and Jared's face fell, "what if there are more goblins out there? I don't know if we could stop them. What if they got in the house? Or grabbed Mom?"

Jared shook his head. If Mallory and Simon destroyed the Guide, then everything they'd done would have been for nothing! "What if we give back the Guide and they keep coming after us?"

"Why would they do that?" Mallory demanded.

"We'd still *know* about the Guide," said Jared. "And we'd still know faeries are real. They might think we'd make another Guide."

"I'd make sure you didn't," said Mallory.

Jared turned to Simon, who was pushing a wooden spoon through the half-frozen mess of meat and cereal. "And what about the griffin? The goblins wanted Byron, didn't they? Are we going to give him back too?"

"No," said Simon, looking out of the faded curtains into the yard. "We can't let Byron go. He isn't all the way better."

"No one is looking for Byron," Mallory said. "It isn't the same thing at all."

Jared tried to think of something that would convince them, something that would prove that they needed the Guide. He didn't understand the faeries any more than Simon or Mallory did. He didn't even know why the faeries would *want* the field guide when the only thing in it was stuff about them. Did the faeries just not want *people* to see it? The only person who might know the answer was Arthur and he was long dead. Jared stopped at that thought.

"There is someone we could ask—someone who really might know what to do," Jared said.

"Who?" asked Simon and Mallory in unison.

Jared had won. The book was safe—at least for now.

He smirked. "Aunt Lucinda."

It looked more like a manor than an asylum.

Chapter Two

IN WHICH Many People Are Mad

"It's very sweet of you kids to want to visit your great-aunt," Mom said, smiling into the rearview mirror at Jared and Simon. "I know she's going to love the cookies you made."

Outside the car window the trees streamed by, patches of yellow and red leaves between bare branches.

"They didn't *make* them," Mallory said. "All they did was arrange frozen dough on a pan."

Jared kicked the back of her seat, hard.

"Hey," Mallory said, turning around and trying to grab her brothers. Jared and Simon

15

snickered. She couldn't quite get them with her seat belt on.

"Well, that's more than you did," their mother said. "You are still grounded, young lady. All three of you have a week left."

"I was at fencing practice," Mallory said, slumping in her seat and rolling her eyes. Jared wasn't sure, but it seemed like there was something odd about the way her ears got pink when she said it.

Jared absently touched his backpack, feeling the outline of the field guide within, safe and sound, wrapped in a towel. So long as he kept it with him, there was no way that Mallory could get rid of it and no way the faeries could take it. Besides, maybe Aunt Lucinda knew about the Guide. Maybe she was the one who'd locked it up in the false bottom of the chest for him to find. If so, maybe she could convince his

brother and sister that it was important enough to keep.

The hospital where their great-aunt lived was huge. It looked more like a manor than an asylum, with massive, redbrick walls, dozens of windows, and a neatly mown lawn. A wide, white stone path edged in rust-and-gold mums led to an entranceway cut from stone. At least ten chimneys rose from the black roof.

"Wow, this place looks older than our house," Simon said.

"Older," said Mallory, "but not nearly as crappy."

"Mallory!" their mother cautioned.

Gravel crunched under their tires as they pulled into the parking lot. Their mother chose a spot next to a battered, green car and turned off the engine.

"Does Aunt Lucy know we're coming?" Simon asked.

"I called ahead," said Mrs. Grace, opening the car door and reaching for her purse. "I don't know how much they tell her, though, so don't be disappointed if she's not expecting us."

"I bet we're the first visitors she's had in a long time," Jared said.

His mother gave him a *look*. "First of all, that is not a nice thing to say, and second, why are you wearing your shirt inside out?"

Jared looked down and shrugged.

"Grandma visits, doesn't she?" Mallory asked.

Their mother nodded. "She comes, but it's hard for her. Lucy was more like a sister than a cousin. And then when she started to . . . deteriorate . . . Grandma was the one who had to take care of things."

Jared wanted to ask what that meant, but something made him hesitate.

They walked through the wide, walnut doors of the institution. There was a desk in the vestibule, where a uniformed man was sitting, reading a newspaper. He looked up at them and reached for a tan phone.

"Sign in, please." He nodded toward an open binder. "Who're you here to see?"

"Lucinda Spiderwick." Their mother bent over the table and wrote their names.

At the sound of the name the man scowled. Jared decided right then that he didn't like this guy at all.

In a few minutes a nurse in a pink shirt with polka dots appeared. She led them through a maze of off-white hallways filled with stale air and the faint odor of iodine. They passed an empty room where a television flickered, and from somewhere nearby there was the sound of giddy laughter. Jared started to think of the asylums in movies and imagined wild-eyed people in straightjackets, biting at their bonds. He peered through the windowed doors they passed.

In one room a young man in a bathrobe giggled over an upside-down book, while in another a woman sobbed near a window.

Jared tried to avert his eyes from the next door, but he heard someone call, "My dancing partner is here!" Peering in, he saw a wild-haired man press his face against the window.

"Mr. Byrne!" The nurse stepped between Jared and the door.

"It's all your fault," the man said, showing yellow teeth.

"Are you okay?" Mallory asked.

Jared nodded, trying to pretend he wasn't

AUNT LUCINDA

shaking.

"Does that happen often?" Mrs. Grace asked.

"No," answered the nurse. "I'm very sorry. He's usually very quiet."

Before Jared could decide whether this visit was a good idea, the nurse stopped at a closed door, rapped twice, and opened it without waiting for a reply. The room was small and the same not-quite-white color as the hallway. In the center of the room was a hospital bed with a metal headboard, and sitting up in it, with a comforter wrapped around her legs, was one

22

of the oldest women Jared had ever seen. Her long hair was as white as sugar. Her skin was pale, too, almost transparent. Her back was hunched and twisted to one side. A metal stand by the side of her bed held a bag of clear liquid with a long tube that connected to the IV in her arm. But her eyes, when they focused on Jared, were bright and alert.

"Why don't I shut that window, Miss S.?" asked the nurse, moving past a nightstand cluttered with antique photos and knickknacks. "You're going to catch a cold."

"No!" Lucinda barked, and the nurse stopped mid-stride. Then in a gentler voice their great-aunt continued. "Leave it be. I need fresh air."

"Hello, Aunt Lucy," Mom said hesitantly. "Do you remember me? I'm Helen."

The old lady nodded slightly, appearing to

regain her composure. "Of course. Melvina's daughter. Goodness. You're quite a bit older than I remembered."

Jared noticed that his mother looked less than pleased by that observation.

"These are my sons, Jared and Simon," she said. "And this is my daughter, Mallory. We've been staying in your house and the children wanted to meet you."

Aunt Lucy frowned. "The house? It is not safe for you to stay at the house."

"We've had people in to make repairs," Mom said. "And look, the children brought some cookies."

"Lovely." The old woman looked at the plate as though it were piled with cockroaches.

Jared, Simon, and Mallory exchanged glances.

The nurse snorted. "Nothing you can do,"

the nurse said to Mrs. Grace, not seeming to care that Aunt Lucy could hear her. "She won't eat anything while we're watching."

Aunt Lucy narrowed her eyes. "I am not deaf, you know."

"You won't try one?" Mom asked, uncovering the sugar cookies and holding the platter out to Aunt Lucinda.

"I'm afraid not," said the old woman. "I find that I am quite content."

"Perhaps we could talk in the hall," their

"Tell me what's happened."

mother whispered to the nurse. "I had no idea things were still so bad." With a worried look she put the plate on a side table and left the room with the nurse.

Jared grinned at Simon. This was even better than they had hoped. Now they were guaranteed at least a few minutes alone.

"Aunt Lucy," Mallory said, speaking fast. "When you told our mom that the house was dangerous, you didn't mean the construction, did you?"

"You meant the faeries," said Simon.

"It's okay to tell us. We've seen them," Jared put in.

Their aunt smiled at them, but it was a sad smile. "Faeries are *exactly* what I meant," she said, patting the bed beside her. "Come. Sit down, you three. Tell me what's happened."

"Come, my dears."

Chapter Three

IN WHICH Stories Are Told and a Theft Is Discovered

We've seen goblins and a troll and a griffin," Jared told her eagerly as they arranged themselves at the foot of the hospital bed. It was such a relief to be believed. Now if she would just explain how important the Guide was, everything would be okay.

"And Thimbletack," Mallory put in, picking up a cookie and taking a bite. "We've seen him, although we're not sure if he counts as a brownie or a boggart."

"Right," said Jared. "But we need to ask

you something important."

"Thimbletack?" Aunt Lucinda asked, patting Mallory's hand. "I haven't seen him in ages. How is he? The same, I expect. They're all always the same, aren't they?"

"I . . . I don't know," Mallory said.

Aunt Lucy reached into the drawer on her side table and brought out a worn, green cloth bag embroidered with stars. "Thimbletack loved these."

Jared took the bag and peered into it. Silvery jacks next to several stone and clay marbles glinted inside the pouch. "They're his?"

"Oh, no," she said. "They're mine, or they

were, when I was young enough to play with such things. I'd just like him to have them. The poor thing, all alone in that old house. He must be so glad you've come."

Jared didn't think Thimbletack was all that glad, but he didn't say so.

"Was Arthur your dad?" Simon asked.

"Yes. Yes, he was," she said with a sigh. "Have you seen his paintings in the house?"

They nodded.

"He was a wonderful artist. He used to illustrate advertisements for soda pop and women's stockings. He made paper dolls for Melvina and me. We had a whole folder of them, with different dresses for each season. I wonder what ever happened to those things."

Jared shrugged. "Maybe they're in the attic."

"It doesn't matter. He's been gone for a long

time now. I'm not sure I'd want to see them anyway."

"Why not?" Simon asked.

"Brings back memories. He left us, you know." She looked down at her thin hands. They were trembling. "He went out for a walk one day and never came back. Mother said she had known he was going to leave for a long time."

Jared was surprised. He'd never given much thought to what Uncle Arthur was like. He thought of the stern, bespectacled face in the library painting. He'd wanted to like his great-great-uncle, who could draw and see faeries. But if what Lucinda said was true, then he didn't like Arthur at all.

"Our dad left too," said Jared.

"I just wish I knew *why*." Aunt Lucy turned her head away, but Jared thought he saw the

glint of tears in her eyes. She pressed her hands together to make them stop shaking.

"Maybe he had to move for his job," Simon offered. "Like our dad."

"Oh, come on, Simon," Jared said. "You can't really believe that load of crap."

"Shut up, morons." Mallory glared at them. "Aunt Lucy, how come you're in this hospital? I mean, you're not crazy."

Jared winced, sure that Aunt Lucy would be mad, but she only laughed. His anger faded.

33

"After Father left, Mother and I moved one town over to live with her brother. I grew up alongside my cousin Melvina—that's your grandmother. I told her about Thimbletack and about the little sprites, but I don't think she ever really believed me.

"Mother died when I was only sixteen. A year later I moved back into the estate. I tried to use what little money there was to fix the place up. Thimbletack was still there, of course, but there were other things too. Sometimes I saw shapes skulking around in the dark. Then one day they stopped hiding. They thought I had Father's book. They would pinch me and poke me and insist that I give it to them. But I didn't have it. Father had taken it with him. He never would have left it behind."

Jared started to speak, but his aunt was lost in her memories and didn't seem to notice.

"One night the faeries brought me a piece of fruit—just a little thing—the size of a grape and red as a rose. They promised not to hurt me anymore. Stupid girl that I was, I took the fruit and sealed my fate."

"Was it poison?" Jared asked, thinking of Snow White and apples.

"Of a fashion," she said with a strange smile. "It tasted better than any food I'd ever imagined. It tasted the way I thought flowers might. It tasted like a song you can't quite put a name to. After that, human food—normal food—was like sawdust and ashes. I couldn't make myself eat it. I would have starved."

"But you didn't starve," Mallory said.

"Thanks to the sprites who I played with when I was a child. They fed me and kept me safe." Aunt Lucy smiled beatifically and stretched out one hand. "Let me introduce you.

35

Creatures the size of walnuts.

Come, my dears, come and see my niece and nephews."

There was a buzzing outside her open window and what had seemed like floating dust in the sunlight suddenly became creatures the size of walnuts, whirring in on iridescent wings. They alighted on the old woman, tangling in her white hair and crawling up the headboard.

"Aren't they darling?" their aunt asked. "My sweet little friends."

Jared knew what they were—sprites, like the ones in the woods—but that didn't make it any less eerie to watch them swarm over his aunt. Simon, however, seemed transfixed.

Mallory spoke, breaking the hush that had settled over them. "I still don't understand who put you here."

"Oh yes, the hospital," said Aunt Lucy. "Your grandmother Melvina became convinced I wasn't well. First she saw the bruises and then the lack of appetite. Then something happened. I don't want to frighten you—no, that's not quite true. I do want you to be frightened. I want you to understand how important it is for you to get out of that house.

"See these marks?" The old woman held out one thin arm. Scars ran deep in her flesh. Simon gasped. "Late one night the monsters came. Little green things with horrible teeth held me down, while a giant one questioned me. I struggled, and their claws scraped my arms and legs. I told them there was no book, that my father had taken it, but nothing I said made any difference. Before that night, my back was straight. Ever since, I have walked hunched over.

"The marks were the final straw for Melvina. She believed I was cutting myself. She couldn't understand . . . so she sent me here."

One of the faeries, clad only in a spiky, green seedpod, flew close and dropped a piece of fruit on the blanket near Simon. Jared blinked—he had been so wrapped up in the story, he'd nearly forgotten about them. The fruit smelled of fresh grass and honey and was enclosed in a papery skin, but underneath Jared could see the red flesh. Aunt Lucinda stared at it and her lips began to tremble.

"For you," said the little faeries in a unified whisper. Simon picked up the fruit and held it between his fingers.

"You're not going to eat it, are you?" Jared asked. Just looking made his mouth water.

"Of course not," said Simon, but his eyes gleamed greedily.

"Don't," said Mallory.

Simon brought the faerie fruit closer to his

"You're not going to eat it, are you?"

mouth, still turning it. "One bite, just one little taste, wouldn't hurt," he said softly.

Aunt Lucinda's hand shot out and plucked the fruit from Simon's fingers. She popped it into her mouth and closed her eyes.

"Hey," said Simon indignantly, jumping up. Then he looked around, disoriented. "What just happened?"

Jared looked at their great-aunt. Her hands were shaking, even as she clasped them in her lap.

"They mean well," she said. "They just don't understand the craving. To them it is only food."

Jared looked at the little faeries. He wasn't sure what they knew or didn't know.

"But now you see why the house is too dangerous for you children. You must get your mother to understand, to leave. If they know you're there, they'll think you have the Guide, and they will never leave you in peace."

"But we do have the Guide," Jared said. "That's what we came here to ask you about."

Aunt Lucy gasped. "You can't possibly—"

"We followed the clues in the library," Jared explained.

"See, she *does* think we should get rid of it!" Mallory said.

"The library? That means . . ." Aunt Lucy looked at him with dawning horror. "If you have the Guide, you have to get out of the house. Immediately! Do you understand me?"

"The Guide's right here." Jared unzipped his backpack and took out the towel-covered book. But when he unwrapped it, the field guide wasn't inside. They were all looking down at an old, worn copy of a cookbook, *Microwave Magic*.

Jared turned to Mallory. "You! You stole it!" He dropped the backpack and went at her with both fists.

Made their way into Arthur's library.

Chapter Four

IN WHICH the Grace Children Look for a Friend

J ared pressed his face up to the car window and tried to pretend that he wasn't crying. The tears fell, hot against his cheeks. He let them run down the cool glass.

He hadn't actually hit Mallory. Simon had grabbed his arms while Mallory kept insisting that she hadn't taken the Guide. All the shouting had brought their mother in. She had dragged them out of there, with lots of apologizing to the nurse and even to Aunt Lucy, who had to be sedated. On the way to the car his mom had told Jared he was lucky the people at the institution didn't lock *him* up.

"Jared," Simon whispered, putting his hand on his twin's back.

"What?" Jared mumbled without turning.

"Maybe Thimbletack took it?"

Jared swiveled around in his seat. His whole body went tense. The moment he heard it, he knew it had to be true. It was Thimbletack's latest prank and his best revenge.

His insides felt as though they'd been splashed with ice water. Why couldn't he have figured that out for himself? Sometimes he got so angry that it scared him. It was like his mind went blank and his body took over.

When they got home, he slid out of the car and sat down on the back steps instead of going into the house with his mother. Mallory sat down beside him.

"I didn't take it," she said. "Remember when

we believed you? Now you better believe me."

"I know," Jared replied, looking down. "I think it was Thimbletack. I . . . I'm sorry."

"You think Thimbletack stole the Guide?" she asked.

"Simon figured it out," said Jared. "It makes sense. Thimbletack keeps playing pranks on me. This is just the worst one yet."

Simon sat down next to Jared on the stairs. "It'll be okay. We'll find it."

"Look," Mallory said, picking at the hem of her sweater where a thread had unraveled. "It's probably for the best."

"No, it's not," Jared said. "Even you should see that. We can't give back what we don't have! The faeries didn't believe Aunt Lucinda when she said she didn't have the book—why would they believe us?"

Mallory scowled and didn't answer.

"I was thinking," Simon said. "Aunt Lucy said that her dad abandoned them, right? But if the field guide was still hidden in the house, maybe he didn't leave on purpose. She said he would never take off without it."

"Then how come the book was still hidden?" Jared asked. "If faeries captured him, he'd have told them where it was."

"Maybe he split before any faeries could catch him," Mallory said. "Let Lucy catch all the heat. Maybe he knew about the giant thing."

"Arthur wouldn't do that," Jared said. As soon as he said it, however, he wondered if it was true.

"Come on," said Simon. "We're never going to figure this out. Let's go visit Byron. He's probably hungry again, and it will get our minds off the Guide."

Mallory snorted. "Yeah, visiting a griffin living in our barn will definitely make us forget all about a book of supernatural creatures."

Jared smiled vaguely. He couldn't stop thinking about the book, about Aunt Lucy and Arthur, and about himself and Mallory and the anger he didn't know what to do with.

Jared looked over at her. "I'm sorry I tried

to hit you."

Mallory ruffled his hair and stood up. "You hit like a girl anyway."

"I do not," Jared said, but he got up and followed her and Simon inside with a grin.

An old, yellowed piece of paper was lying on the kitchen table. Jared took a step closer. A poem had been scribbled on it.

"Thimbletack," Jared said.

> *Rash child who thinks he's smart*
> *Wondering about your book?*
> *Maybe I'm tearing it apart*
> *Or hiding it where you won't look.*

"Wow, he's really mad," said Simon.

Jared was torn between relief and horror. The book *was* with Thimbletack, but what had he done with it? Had it really been destroyed?

"Hey, I know," Mallory offered hopefully.

"Aunt Lucy's jacks and marbles. We could leave them for him."

"I'll write a note." Simon turned over the paper and scrawled something on the back.

"What does it say?" Mallory asked.

"We're sorry," read Simon.

Jared eyed the note skeptically. "I'm not sure

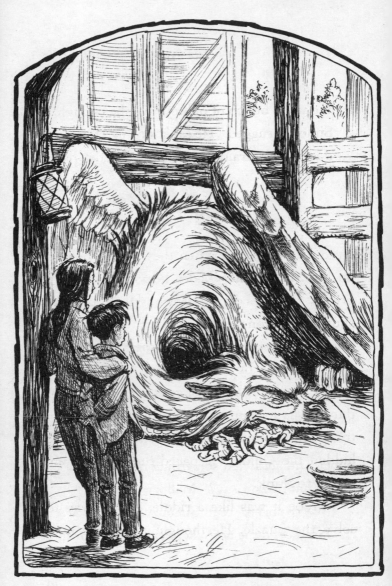

Byron was sleeping.

if that and a bunch of old toys will be enough."

Simon shrugged. "He can't stay mad forever."

Jared was afraid he could do exactly that.

Byron was sleeping when they went to check on him, his feathery sides heaving with each breath. His eyes darted back and forth beneath shut lids. Simon pointed out that they probably shouldn't try to wake him, so they left another plate of meat by his beak and walked back to the house. Mallory suggested a game, but Jared was too nervous to do anything except try to figure out where Thimbletack could have hidden the Guide. He paced the living room, trying to think.

Maybe it was like a riddle, with a way to solve the puzzle. He thought about the note again, turning it over in his mind, looking for clues.

"It can't be inside the walls." Mallory sat cross-legged on the couch. "It's too big. How could he get it in there?"

"There are lots of rooms we've never even been in," Simon said, perching next to her. "Lots of places we haven't looked."

Jared stopped mid-stride. "Wait. What about right in front of us?"

"What?" asked Simon.

"In Arthur's library! There are so many books up there, we would never notice it."

"Hey, that's true," Mallory said.

"Yeah," said Simon. "And even if the Guide isn't there—who knows what else we'll find."

The three went upstairs into the hall and opened the closet door. Crouching down, Jared crawled through the secret passage underneath the lowest shelf and made his way into Arthur's library. The walls were lined with bookshelves, except for where a large painting of their great-uncle hung. Despite their many visits to the library, dust still covered most of the bookshelves, a testament to how few of the volumes had been inspected closely.

Mallory and Simon scrambled in behind him.

"Where do we start?" Simon asked, looking around.

"You take the desk," Mallory said. "Jared, you take that bookshelf, and I'll take the one over here."

Jared nodded and tried to brush off some of the dust on the first shelf. The books were as strange as he remembered from previous trips to the library: *Physiognomy of Wings, Impact of Scales on Musculature, Venoms of the World,* and *Details of Draconite.* When Jared had first looked at them, however, there had been a kind of awe that was absent now. He felt numb. The book was gone, Thimbletack hated him, and Arthur wasn't the person he'd imagined. It was a cheat—all this magic. It seemed so great, but underneath, it was just as disappointing as everything else.

Jared glanced over at the painting of Arthur hanging on the wall. He didn't even *look* nice to Jared anymore. The Arthur in the painting was thin-lipped with a crease between his brows that Jared now figured was annoyance. He was probably thinking about leaving his family even then.

Jared's vision blurred and his eyes burned. It was stupid to cry over someone he'd never met, but he couldn't help it.

"Did you sketch this?" Simon called from the desk.

He didn't even look nice.

Jared wiped his face against his sleeve, hoping his twin didn't notice the tears. "Just toss it."

"No," Simon said. "It's good. It really looks like Dad."

Learning to draw had been another stupid idea. All it had done was get him in trouble at school for doodling instead of working. He walked to the desk and tore the drawing in half, crumpling it in his fists. "*Just toss it!*"

"Guys," Mallory said. "Come here."

Mallory held several rolled-up sheets of paper and two long, metal tubes. "Look." She knelt down and began unrolling pages on the floor.

The boys crouched around. There, sketched in pencils and painted in watercolors, was a map of their neighborhood. Some places didn't look quite right—there were more houses and more roads now—but there were a lot of places they still recognized. The notes, however, were a surprise.

There was a thin circle surrounding a stretch of forest behind their house, with letters printed inside the circle. "TROLL HUNTING TERRITORY," Simon read.

Mallory groaned. "If only we'd had this before!"

Along a stretch of road near an old quarry, DWARVES? was written, while a tree not far from the house was clearly marked SPRITES. The strangest thing, however, was a note on the

The boys crouched around.

edge of the hills, close to their house. It looked like it had been written hastily, as the handwriting was sloppy. It read, "September 14th. Five o'clock. Bring the remains of the book."

"What do you think it's about?" Simon asked.

"Could 'the book' mean the field guide?" Jared wondered aloud.

Mallory shook her head. "Could be, but the Guide was still here."

They looked at each other for a moment in silence.

"When did Arthur disappear?" Jared finally asked.

Simon shrugged. "Probably only Aunt Lucy would remember."

"So either he went to the meeting and never came back," Mallory said, "or he took off and never went to the meeting at all."

"We have to show this to Aunt Lucinda!" Jared said.

His sister shook her head. "It doesn't prove anything. It'll just make her more upset."

"But maybe he didn't mean to leave," Jared said with a scowl. "Don't you think she deserves to know that?"

"Let's go and look ourselves," Simon said. "We can follow the map and see where it leads. Maybe there'll be some clue about what really happened."

Jared hesitated. He wanted to go. He had been on the verge of suggesting it himself when Simon had spoken. Yet now he couldn't stop himself from wondering if it was some kind of a trap.

"Following this map would be really, really dumb," said Mallory. "*Especially* if we think something might have happened to him out there."

"That map is so old, Mallory," Simon said. "What could happen?"

"Famous last words," Mallory said, but she traced the hills on the map thoughtfully with her fingers.

"It's the only way we will ever find out anything," said Jared.

Mallory sighed. "I guess we could take a look. As long as it's daytime. But the first weird thing we see, we go back. Agreed?"

"Agreed," Jared said with a smile.

Simon started to roll up the map. "Agreed," he said.

A summer breeze blew across the hill.

Chapter Five

IN WHICH There Are Many Riddles and Few Answers

To Jared's surprise, their mother agreed to let them go for a short walk. She blamed their constant squabbling on being cooped up inside but, with a single stern look at Jared, made all three promise to be back before dark. Mallory grabbed her fencing sword, Jared got his backpack and a new notebook, and Simon brought a butterfly net from the library.

"What is that for?" Mallory asked as they crossed Dulac Drive, following the map.

"To catch things," Simon said, without

looking at her directly.

"What kind of *things*? Don't you have enough animals?"

Simon shrugged.

"You bring home one new creature and I'm feeding it to Byron."

"Hey," Jared said, interrupting them. "Which direction?"

Simon studied the map, then pointed.

Simon, Mallory, and Jared made their way up the steep hillside. Trees were sparse, their trunks growing on a slant between patches of grass and moss-covered boulders. For a long while they just climbed, not really talking. Jared thought that this might be a nice place to bring his sketchbook sometime—but then he remembered that he'd given up on drawing.

Near the top of the hill the land leveled out and the trees grew thicker. Simon turned around suddenly and started leading them back down the hill.

"Where are we going?" Jared asked.

Simon waved the map at him. "This is the way," he said.

Mallory nodded as though she didn't think it was unusual that they were retracing their steps.

"Are you sure?" Jared asked. "I don't think so."

"I'm *sure*," Simon said.

Right then a summer breeze blew across the hill, and Jared thought he heard a chorus of laughter from beneath their feet. He stumbled and almost fell.

"Did you hear that?"

"What?" Simon asked, looking around nervously.

Jared shrugged. He was sure he had heard something, but now there was only silence.

A little bit down the path Simon changed direction again. He started walking back up and to the right. Mallory followed amiably.

"Where are we heading now?" Jared asked. They were going up again, toward the top of the first hill, which was good—but they had been traveling at such an angle that Jared didn't think they could be anywhere close to the meeting spot on the map.

"I know what I'm doing," said Simon. Mallory followed without question, which bothered Jared almost as much as the zigzag pattern Simon was taking. He wished he had the Guide. He tried to go through the pages in his mind, looking for some explanation. He recalled something about people losing their way, even really close to home. . . .

Jared began to poke the grass he stepped on with his shoe. One tall weed scuttled to the side.

"Stray sod!" He thought of the entry in the Guide. Suddenly it made sense that only he had noticed they were going in the wrong direction. "Simon! Mallory! Turn your shirts inside out like mine!"

"No," Simon said. "I know the way. Why do you always have to boss me around?"

"It's a faerie trick!" Jared yelled.

"Forget it. You follow me for a change!"

"Just do it, Simon!"

"No! Didn't you hear me? No!"

THE PHOOKA

Jared tackled his brother, causing both of them to land on the grass. Jared tried to rip off his brother's sweater, but Simon was hugging his arms to his sides.

"Stop it, both of you!" Mallory pushed them apart. Then, to Jared's surprise, she sat down on Simon and tugged off his sweater. He immediately noticed that she'd already turned her own inside out.

A strange expression came over Simon's face as his inside-out sweater was shoved back over his head. "Wow. Where are we?"

70

A peal of laughter rang out from above their heads.

"Most don't make it this far—or this near, depending," said a creature perched in the tree. It had the body of a monkey with short, blackish brown speckled fur and a long tail that curled around the branch on which it sat. A thick ruff of fur surrounded its neck, but its face was rabbity, with long ears and whiskers.

"Depending on what?" Jared asked. He wasn't sure if he should be amused or afraid.

Suddenly the creature swung his head upside down so that its ears brushed its belly and its chin pointed toward the sky. "Clever is as clever does."

Jared jumped.

Mallory swung her rapier out in front of her. "Stay where you are!"

"Goodness, a beast with a sword," it hissed.

"Most don't make it this far."

Swinging its head right-ways-round again, it blinked twice. "I wonder if it's mad. Swords haven't been the fashion for ages!"

"We're not beasts," said Jared defensively.

"What are you then?" asked the creature.

"I'm a boy," said Jared. "And, well, that's my sister. A girl."

"That's no girl," it said. "Where's her dress?"

"Dresses haven't been the fashion for ages," Mallory said with a smirk.

"We answered your questions," Jared said. "Now answer ours. What are *you*?"

"The Black Dog of the Night," declared the creature proudly, before its head spun around once more, peering at them with one eye open. "An ass or perhaps merely a sprite."

"What does that mean?" demanded Mallory. "It's just stupid."

"I think it's a phooka!" said Jared. "Yes, I

remember now. They're shape shifters."

"Are they dangerous?" asked Simon.

"Very!" said the phooka, nodding vigorously.

"I'm not sure," Jared said, under his breath. Then, clearing his throat, he addressed the creature. "We were looking for some trace of our great-uncle."

"You've lost your uncle! How careless."

Jared sighed and tried to decide if the phooka was as crazy as it seemed. "Well, he's been gone a long time, actually. Close to seventy years. We're just hoping to find out what happened to him."

"Anyone can live that long—all they have to do is keep from dying. But I understand that humans live much longer in captivity than they do in the wild."

"What?" Jared asked.

"When looking for something," said the phooka, "one ought to be sure one wants to find it."

"Oh, never mind!" Mallory said. "Let's just keep going."

"Let's at least ask it what's in the valley up ahead," said Simon.

Mallory rolled her eyes. "Oh, yeah, like it's going to start making sense."

Simon ignored her. "Can you please tell us what's up ahead? We were following this map until we got turned around by the moving grass."

"If grass can move," said the phooka, "then a boy could find himself rooted in place."

"Please, please, just stop encouraging it," said Mallory.

"Elves," said the phooka, eyeing Mallory as though affronted. "Shall I be direct when I direct you into the direct path of the elves?"

"What do they want?" asked Jared.

"They have what you want and they want

what you have," said the phooka.

Mallory groaned audibly.

"We said we'd turn back when things got weird." Mallory pointed at the phooka with her rapier. "And that thing is about as weird as it gets."

"But not bad." Jared looked toward the hills. "Let's go on a little farther."

"I don't know," Mallory said. "What about those grass things and us getting lost?"

"The phooka said that the elves have what we want!"

Simon nodded. "We're really close, Mal."

Mallory sighed. "I don't like this, but I'd rather we were the ones sneaking up on them."

They started walking down the hill, away from the road.

"Wait! Come back," called the phooka. "There is something I must tell you."

They turned back.

"What is it?" Jared asked.

"Bonny nonny bonny," said the phooka with precision.

"Is that what you wanted to tell us?"

"No, not at all," said the phooka.

"Well, what then?" Jared demanded.

"What an author doesn't know could fill a

They stopped in a meadow.

book," said the phooka. With that, his body toed its way up the tree until it was gone.

The three children made their way slowly down the other side of the hill. As the trees thickened once more, they noticed how quiet the woods had become. No birds sang in the trees. There seemed to be only the rustle of grass and the snap of twigs under their feet.

They stopped in a meadow ringed by trees. At the center a single, tall thorn tree stood, surrounded by fat white-and-red toadstools.

"Uh," Jared said.

"Right. Weird. Let's get out of here," Mallory said.

But as they turned, the trees wove together, branches entwining with other branches, lacing into a fence of foliage that reached down to the earthen floor of the glade.

"Oh, crap," said Mallory.

Three beings stepped out.

Chapter Six

IN WHICH Jared
Fulfills the Phooka's Prediction

Across the grove the branches parted and three beings stepped out from the trees. They were about Mallory's size, with freckled skin browned by sunlight. The first was a woman with apple green eyes and a green sheen across her shoulders and at her temples. Leaves were tangled in her tousled hair. The second was a man with what looked like small horns along his brow. His skin was flushed a deeper green than the woman's skin and he held a gnarled staff in his hands. The third elf had thick, red hair woven with red berries and two large seedpods that stuck up on either side of his head. His skin was brown, speckled with red at his throat.

"These are elves?" Simon asked.

"No one has followed this path for a long time," said the green-eyed elf as though no one had spoken. She held her head high, like one accustomed to being obeyed. "All who might have stumbled into this grove have been led astray. But here they are. How curious."

"The grass," Jared whispered to his brother.

"They must have it," the red-haired elf declared to his companions. "How else would they come this way? How else would they discover the means to stay on the path?" He turned to the three children. "I am Lorengorm. We would bargain with you."

"For what?" Jared asked, hoping his voice wouldn't shake. The elves were beautiful, but

the only emotion he could
read on their faces was
a strange hunger that
unnerved him.

"You want your
freedom," said the
elf with what had
looked like horns.
Jared realized that
they were actual-
ly leaves. "We want
Arthur's book."

"Freedom from what?"
Mallory asked.

THE LEAF-HORNED ELF

The leaf-horned elf indicated the border
of trees with one hand and smiled an unkind
smile. "We will guest you until you tire of our
hospitality."

"Arthur didn't give you the book. Why

should we?" Jared hoped they couldn't tell that he was guessing.

The leaf-horned elf sniffed. "We have long known that mankind is brutal. Once, at least, humans were ignorant. Now we would keep knowledge of our existence from you to protect ourselves."

"You cannot be trusted. You cleave the forests." Lorengorm scowled and his eyes flashed. "Poison the rivers, hunt the griffins from the skies and the serpents from the seas. Imagine what you could do if you knew all of our weaknesses."

"But *we* never did any of those

things!" said Simon.

"And no one even believes in faeries," Jared said. He thought of Lucinda. "No one sane, anyway."

Lorengorm's laugh sounded hollow. "There are few enough faeries left to believe in. We make our homes in the sparse forests left to us. Soon even those will be gone."

The green-eyed elf lifted one hand toward the woven wall of branches. "Let me show you."

Jared noticed all types of faeries, sitting in the circle of trees, peering through the gaps in the

85

wood. Their black eyes glittered, their wings buzzed, and their mouths moved, but none entered the grove. It felt like a trial, with the elves acting as both judge and jury. Then a few branches untwined and something else stepped through.

It was white and the size of a deer. Its fur was ivory and its long mane hung in tangles. The horn that jutted from its forehead was twisted to an end that looked sharp. It lifted its wet nose and scented the air. As it approached them the valley went quiet. Even the creature's own steps were noiseless. It didn't look at all tame.

Mallory stepped toward it, tilting her head slightly and extending her hand.

"Mallory," Jared warned. "Don't . . ."

But she was beyond hearing, stretching out her fingers to pet the creature's flank. It stayed completely still, and Jared was afraid to even breathe as Mallory stroked the unicorn's side, then tangled her hand in its mane. As she did, the bone horn touched her forehead and her eyes closed. Then her whole body began to tremble.

"Mallory!" Jared said.

Beneath the lids Mallory's eyes darted back and forth, as though she were dreaming. Then she staggered to her knees.

Jared ran forward to grab her. Simon was only a step behind him. When Jared touched Mallory, he was drawn into the vision.

Everything soundless.

Knots of blackberry bushes. Men on horseback. Lean dogs with red tongues. A glimmer of white, and a unicorn bursts through the glade, legs already dark with mud. Arrows fly, burying themselves in white flesh. The unicorn bellows and goes down in a cloud of

Her whole body began to tremble.

leaves. Dog teeth rip skin. A man with a knife hacks the horn from the head while the unicorn is still moving.

The images came faster then, more disjointed. *A girl in a colorless gown, urged on by hunters, lures the unicorn closer. One stray arrow knocks her to the ground. She falls, pale arm slung over pale flank. Both are still. Then hundreds of gory horns, shaped into goblets, crushed into charms and powders. White pelts streaked with blood, stacked in a pile buzzing with black flies.*

Jared pulled free of the dream, his stomach heaving. To his surprise Mallory was crying, her tears darkening the white fur. Simon put an awkward hand on the unicorn's side.

The unicorn tipped its head forward, nuzzling Mallory's hair with its lips.

"It really likes you," Simon said. He looked a little annoyed. Animals usually liked him best.

Mallory shrugged. "I'm a girl."

"We know what you saw," the leaf-horned elf said. "Give us the Guide. It must be destroyed."

"What about the goblins?" demanded Jared.

"What of them? The goblins love your world," said Lorengorm. "Your machines and poisons have made a haven for their kind."

"You seemed fine with using them to try to take the book from us," Jared said.

"We?" asked the green-eyed elf, her eyes wide and her mouth hard. "You think that we would send such sentries? It is Mulgarath that commands them."

"Who is Mulgarath?" Mallory stood up, still petting the unicorn absently.

"An ogre," said Lorengorm. "He has been gathering goblins to him and making pacts with dwarves. We think he wants Arthur Spiderwick's Guide for himself."

"Why?" Jared asked. "Don't you know everything that's inside it?"

The elves exchanged uncomfortable glances. Finally the leaf-horned elf spoke. "We make art. We do not feel the need to cut things apart to see what they're made of. What Arthur Spiderwick did, none of our kind would do."

The green-eyed elf put a hand on the other

elf's shoulder. "What he means is that there may be things in the Guide that we do not know."

Jared thought for a moment. "So you don't really care about humans getting Arthur's field guide. You just don't want Mulgarath to have it!"

"The book is dangerous in anyone's hands," said the green-eyed elf. "There is too much knowledge therein. Give it over to us. It will be destroyed and you will be rewarded."

Jared held out his hands. "We don't have it," he said. "We couldn't give it to you if we wanted to."

The leaf-horned elf shook his head and slammed the butt of his staff. "You lie!"

"We really don't have it," said Mallory. "Honest."

Lorengorm raised a single, red brow. "Then

where is it?"

"We think the house brownie has it," Simon put in. "But we're not sure."

"You lost it?" The green-eyed elf gasped.

"Thimbletack probably has it," Jared said in a small voice.

"We have tried to be reasonable," said the leaf-horned elf. "Humans are faithless."

"Faithless?" Jared repeated. "How do we know we can trust *you*?" He snatched the map from Simon and held it up for the elves to see. "We found this. It was Arthur's. It looks like he came here and I guess he met you. I want to know what you did with him."

"We spoke with Arthur," said the leaf-horned elf. "He thought to trick us. He had sworn he would destroy the Guide, and he came to our meeting with a bag of blackened paper and ashes. But he lied. He had burned another book. The Guide remained unharmed."

"We honor our word," said the green-eyed elf. "Though it be bitter, we fulfill our pledges. We have no sympathy for those who would deceive us."

"What did you do?" asked Jared.

"We kept him from doing further harm," said the green-eyed elf.

"Now you have come," said the leaf-horned elf. "And you *will* bring us the Guide."

Lorengorm waved his hand, and pale roots crept from the ground. Jared cried out, but his voice was lost in the creaking of branches and shuffling of leaves. The trees were untwining, their limbs moving back into natural shapes. But dirty, hairy roots climbed Jared's legs and held him.

"Bring us the Guide or your brother will remain trapped forever in Faerie," said the leaf-horned elf.

Jared had no doubt that he meant it.

"Jared, *help!*" Jared called.

Chapter Seven

IN WHICH Jared Is Finally Pleased to Have a Twin

Mallory leapt forward, brandishing her rapier. Simon held his net in awkward imitation. The unicorn shook its head, mane flying as it galloped noiselessly into the depths of the forest.

"Oh ho!" said the leaf-horned elf. "Now we see the true character of humans!"

"Let my brother go!" Mallory yelled.

Jared suddenly had an idea.

"*Jared*, help!" Jared called, hoping that Simon and Mallory would get the hint.

Simon just looked at him in confusion.

"*Jared,*" said Jared, "you have to help me."

Then Simon smiled at him, his eyes lighting up with understanding. "*Simon,* are you okay?"

"I'm fine, *Jared.*" Jared pulled his leg against the grip of the roots with all his might. "But I can't move."

"We'll come back with the Guide, *Simon,*" Simon said, "and then they'll have to let you go."

"No," said Jared. "If you come back, they might keep us all hostage. Make them promise!"

"Our word is our bond," sniffed the green-eyed elf.

"You didn't give us your word," Mallory said, looking at her brothers with growing alarm.

"Promise that Jared and Mallory can leave the grove safely and that if they return, they will not be held against their will," said Jared.

Mallory looked ready to protest, but she remained silent.

The elves looked at the siblings with some hesitation. Finally Lorengorm nodded. "Let it be so. Jared and Mallory may go from this grove. They will not be held here against their will now or later. Should they not bring the Guide, we will keep their brother, Simon, for all time. He will remain with us, ageless, beneath the hill, for a hundred times a hundred years—and should he ever leave, one step on the ground will bring all the missing years on to him at once."

The real Simon shivered and took a step closer to Mallory.

"Go swiftly," said the elf.

Mallory looked searchingly at Jared. The tip of her rapier had dipped, but she was still holding it in front of her and she made no

They turned and looked back at him.

move to leave the grove. Jared tried to smile encouragingly, but he was scared and he knew it showed on his face.

Shaking her head, Mallory followed Simon. After a few paces they turned and looked back at him, then started climbing the steep hill. In a few minutes they were obscured by leaves. Jared spoke.

"You have to let me go," he said.

"And why is that?" asked the leaf-horned elf. "You have heard our promise. We will not release you until your brother and sister have brought us the Guide."

Jared shook his head. "You said you wouldn't release *Simon*. I'm Jared."

"What?" demanded Lorengorm.

The leaf-horned elf took a step toward Jared, his hands curled like claws.

Jared swallowed hard. "Your word is your

bond. You have to let me go."

"Prove yourself, child," said the green-eyed elf. Her lips pressed in a thin line.

"Here." Jared shrugged off his backpack into his trembling hands. There, along the top, three letters were monogrammed into the red canvas: JEG. "See. Jared Evan Grace."

"Go," said the leaf-horned elf, speaking the

word as though it were a curse. "Much may your freedom please you if we come upon you or your false-hearted siblings again."

With that, the roots untwined from Jared's legs. He ran from the grove as fast as he could. He did not look back.

As he reached the top of the hill, he heard laughter.

He looked up into the nearby trees, but there was no sign of the phooka. Still, Jared was only half surprised when its now-familiar voice spoke. "I see you didn't find your uncle. A pity. Were you a little less clever, perhaps you'd have had more success."

Jared shuddered and rushed down the other side of the hill, fast enough that he was barely able to stop from running out into the middle of the road. He crossed the street and ran through the iron gates into his own front-

He heard laughter.

yard, panting.

Mallory and Simon were waiting for him on the steps. His sister said nothing but embraced him in a very un-Mallory-like fashion. He let himself be hugged.

"I had no idea what you were going to do," said Simon with a laugh. "That was a great trick."

"Thanks for going along with it," Jared said with a grin. "The phooka said something to me on the way back."

"Anything that made any sense?" Mallory asked.

"Well, I was thinking," said Jared. "Remember how the elves said they'd keep me in Faerie?"

"Keep *you*?" asked Simon. "They said *Simon*."

"Yeah, but think of what they were going to

do. They were going to keep me there forever. Ageless, remember? Forever."

"So you think . . ." Mallory's voice trailed off.

"When I was leaving, the phooka said that if I'd been less clever, I might have had more success finding my uncle."

"You mean Arthur could be trapped with the elves?" asked Simon as they trudged up the

steps to the house.

"I think so," Jared said.

"Then he's still alive," Mallory said.

Jared opened the back door and stepped into the mudroom. He was still shaking from his encounter with the elves, but the smile on his face grew. Maybe Arthur hadn't run out on his family. Maybe he was a prisoner of the elves. And maybe—if Jared was clever enough—Arthur could even be saved.

Daydreaming about rescue, he barely noticed the glimmer of silver at his feet before he fell. Something sharp pressed into Jared's thigh and outstretched hand. Simon tripped too, crashing onto Jared, and Mallory, only a couple of steps behind, went down on top of them both.

"Crap!" yelled Jared, looking around. The floor was littered with jacks and marbles.

"Ow," said Simon, trying to squirm out from under his sister. "Get off me, Mal."

"Ow yourself," Mallory said, pushing herself to her feet. "I'm gonna kill that little boggart." She paused. "You know what, Jared? If we find Arthur's field guide, I say we keep it."

Jared looked back at her. "You do?"

She nodded. "I don't know about you two, but I'm tired of being bossed around by faeries."

End of

BOOK THREE

About TONY DiTERLIZZI . . .

A *New York Times* best-selling author, Tony DiTerlizzi created the Zena Sutherland Award–winning *Ted, Jimmy Zangwow's Out-of-This-World Moon Pie Adventure*, as well as illustrations in Tony Johnston's Alien and Possum beginning-reader series. Most recently, his brilliantly cinematic version of Mary Howitt's classic *The Spider and the Fly* was awarded a Caldecott Honor. In addition, Tony's art has graced the work of such well-known fantasy names as J.R.R. Tolkien, Anne McCaffrey, Peter S. Beagle, and Greg Bear as well as Wizards of the Coast's *Magic The Gathering*. He and his wife, Angela, reside with their pug, Goblin, in Amherst, Massachusetts. Visit Tony on the World Wide Web at www.diterlizzi.com.

and HOLLY BLACK

An avid collector of rare folklore volumes, Holly Black spent her early years in a decaying Victorian mansion where her mother fed her a steady diet of ghost stories and books about faeries. Accordingly, her first novel, *Tithe: A Modern Faerie Tale*, is a gothic and artful glimpse at the world of Faerie. Published in the fall of 2002, it received two starred reviews and a Best Book for Young Adults citation from the American Library Association. She lives in West Long Branch, New Jersey, with her husband, Theo, and a remarkable menagerie. Visit Holly on the World Wide Web at www.blackholly.com.

Tony and Holly continue to work day and night fending off angry faeries and goblins in order to bring the Grace children's story to you.

A boggart, then goblins,
now wood elves, oh my!
What else will the Grace kids
unearth by and by?

JARED GRACE

All eyes on Jared.
This magnet, for trouble,
will soon have his very own
twin seeing double.

And beneath the Old Quarry
just outside of town
lives a king with a kingdom.
But who wears the crown?

Be bold, keep reading,
but beware the path down.

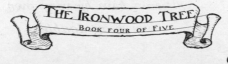

THE IRONWOOD TREE
BOOK FOUR OF FIVE

Chapter One

IN WHICH There Is Both a Fight and a Duel

The engine of the station wagon was already running. Mallory leaned against the door, her everyday sneakers grungy against the bright white of her long fencing socks. Her hair was gelled and pulled back into a ponytail so tight that it made her eyes bulge. Mrs. Grace stood on the driver's side, her hands on her hips.

"I found him!" Jared panted, running up to join them.

"Simon," their mother called. "Where were you? We looked everywhere!"

"The carriage house," Simon said. "Taking care of the . . . uh, a bird I found." Simon looked uncomfortable. He wasn't used to having to lie. That was mostly Jared's job.

Mallory rolled her eyes. "Too bad Mom wouldn't leave without you."

"Mallory," their mother said, shaking her head in disapproval. "All of you—get in the car. We're going to be late already, and I still have to drop something off."

As Mallory turned to put her bag in the trunk, Jared noticed that her chest looked strange. Stiff and weirdly . . . big.

"What are you wearing?" he asked, pointing.

"Shut up," she said.

He snickered. "It's just that you look like you've got—"

"Shut up!" she said again, getting into the front seat of the car while the boys climbed in the back. "It's for protection, and I have to have it on."

Jared smiled against the window and watched the woods go by. There hadn't been any faerie activity in more than two weeks—even Thimbletack had been quiet—and occasionally Jared had to remind himself that it was real. Sometimes it seemed like everything could be explained away. Even the burning water had been dismissed as simply being from a contaminated well. Until the old plumbing could be connected to a central line, they used gallons of supermarket water without Mom thinking it was weird. But there was Simon's griffin, and *that* couldn't be explained by anything but Arthur's field guide.

"Stop chewing on your ponytail," their mother said to Mallory. "What is making you

JWM

CHRIS-THE-CAPTAIN

so jittery? Is this new team really that good?"

"I'm fine," Mallory said.

Back in New York she'd fenced in sweatpants and a team jacket chosen from a pile. There had been a guy who'd hold up his hand on your side if you had scored. But at the new school, fencers wore real uniforms and had electric rapiers wired to a scoring machine that flashed lights when someone got hit. Jared thought that was enough to make anyone jumpy.

Apparently their mother had another explanation. "It's that boy, isn't it? The one you were talking to on Wednesday when I picked you up."

"What boy?" Simon asked from the backseat, already starting to laugh.

"Be quiet," said their mother, but she answered anyway. "Chris, the fencing captain. He is the captain, isn't he?"

Their sister grunted noncommittally.

"Chris and Mallory sitting in a tree, K-I-S-S-I-N-G," Simon sang. Jared giggled, and Mallory turned toward the backseat, eyes narrowed.

"Want to lose all your baby teeth at once?"

"Don't listen to them," their mother said. "And *don't* worry. You're a smart, pretty girl and a great fencer. I bet he likes you."

"Mom!" Mallory groaned and sank lower in the front seat.

Their mother stopped at the library where she worked, dropped off some paperwork, and

"I bet he likes you."

returned to the idling car, somewhat out of breath.

"Come on! I can't be late," Mallory said, smoothing her hair back unnecessarily. "It's my first match!"

Their mother sighed. "We're almost there."

Jared resumed looking out the window in time to see what looked like a deep crater. They were driving over a stone bridge. The school bus never went this way.

"Simon, look! What's that?"

"It's an abandoned quarry," Mallory said impatiently. "Where people used to dig up rocks."

"A *quarry*," Jared echoed. He remembered something from the map they'd found in their great-uncle Arthur's study.

"Think they found any fossils?" Simon asked, half crawling over Jared to look out the

window. "I wonder what dinosaurs lived in this area."

Their mother was already pulling the car into the school parking lot. She didn't answer.

Jared, Simon, and their mother climbed up onto the gymnasium bleachers while Mallory went to sit with her team. Already seated were a few other families and a smattering of people Jared recognized from school. A rectangular pad was spread out on the floor with lines taped on it. Mallory called it a *piste,* but Jared thought it just looked like a long, black mat. Behind it was a folding table where the score-board sat, its large, colored buttons making it look more like a game than something impor-tant. The director was fiddling with the wires, connecting them to a foil and testing the force needed to make the buzzer sound and the lights flash.

Mallory sat down on a metal chair at one

end of the *piste* and started unpacking her bag. Chris squatted down to talk with Mallory. The other team milled around the opposite end. All the uniforms were so white, they made Jared's eyes hurt.

Finally the director announced it was time for the first bout. He called two fencers up and made each of them strap a small receiver to the back of their pants, then attached cords to their foils. It all looked so professional. As the fencers began, Jared tried to recall what Mallory had said about the flashing lights, but he couldn't.

"This is stupid. I like fencing better without all this junk," Jared said to no one in particular.

Two matches later Jared had figured out that the colored lights meant that the hit was good, but the white light meant that the hit didn't count. Only hits in the chest counted. Which was dumb, really, Jared had always thought. Getting hit in the leg hurt plenty, and Jared had practiced with Mallory enough to know.

Finally Mallory was called to the mat. Her opponent—a tall boy called Daniel Something-or-Other—snickered as he put on his mask. He obviously had no idea what was coming.

Jared elbowed Simon as his brother put a pretzel into his mouth. "He's going to get it."

"Ow," said Simon. "Cut it out."

Mallory's ponytail bounced as she advanced. Her sword struck Daniel hard in the chest before he could parry. The director raised one hand, and the scoreboard lit up with a point for Mallory. Jared grinned.

Their mother was craning her whole body forward as if there were something to hear other than the clang of thin metal blades locked

"I like fencing better without all this junk."

in the pattern of attack, parry, and riposte. Daniel lunged desperately, too upset to control his advance. Mallory countered, turning her defense into an attack and scoring another point.

Their sister beat Daniel without being touched once. They saluted each other formally, and the boy took off his mask, red-faced and breathing hard. When Mallory's mask came off, she smiled, eyes slitted with satisfaction.

On the way back to the metal chairs the fencing captain gave Mallory a quick awkward hug. Jared couldn't see very well, but he could have sworn that Mallory's face flushed darker than it had been when she stepped off the mat.

The bouts went on, with Mallory's team doing pretty well. When it was the captain's turn to fence, Mallory cheered loudly. Unfortunately it didn't seem to help. He was defeated by a narrow margin. Slinking back to his seat, he walked past her without a word and shrugged off her attempts to talk to him.

When Mallory was called to the mat again, Chris didn't even look up.

Jared watched from the stands and scowled. His scowl deepened when he noticed a blond-haired girl in white fencing garb rooting through his sister's bag.

"Who's that?" Jared pointed.

Simon shrugged. "I dunno. She hasn't fenced yet."

Could the girl be a friend of his sister? Maybe she was just borrowing something? The furtive way the girl stopped when anyone from the team looked her way made Jared think she was stealing. But what would anyone want in a bag of Mallory's dirty socks and spare foils?

Clang of thin metal blades.

ACKNOWLEDGMENTS

Tony and Holly would like to thank
Steve and Dianna for their insight,
Starr for her honesty,
Myles and Liza for sharing the journey,
Ellen and Julie for helping make this our reality,
Kevin for his tireless enthusiasm and faith in us,
and especially Angela and Theo—
there are not enough superlatives
to describe your patience
in enduring endless nights
of Spiderwick discussion.

The text type for this book is set in Cochin.
The display types are set in Nevins Hand and Rackham.
The illustrations are rendered in pen and ink.